D

SNOWBOARD
HERO

BY JAKE MADDOX

text by
Brandon Terrell

STONE ARCH BOOKS
a capstone imprint

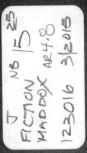

Jake Maddox JV books are published by Stone Arch Books
A Capstone Imprint
1710 Roe Crest Drive
North Mankato, Minnesota 56003
www.capstonepub.com

Library of Congress Cataloging-in-Publication Data

Maddox, Jake, author.
  Snowboard hero / by Jake Maddox ; text by Brandon Terrell.
    pages cm. -- (Jake Maddox JV)
  Summary: Thirteen-year-old Kaleb has always looked up to his older stepbrother, Luke,
in snowboarding and everything else, so when Luke is wounded in Afghanistan Kaleb is
devastated — and to honor his brother he is set on competing on the difficult slopestyle
course.
  ISBN 978-1-4342-9636-8 (library binding) -- ISBN 978-1-4342-9668-9 (pbk.) -- ISBN 978-1-
4965-0177-6 (ebook PDF)
  1. Snowboarding--Juvenile fiction. 2. Stepbrothers--Juvenile fiction. 3. Contests--Juvenile
fiction. 4. Afghan War, 2001---Veterans--Juvenile fiction. 5. Colorado--Juvenile fiction. [1.
Snowboarding--Fiction. 2. Brothers--Fiction. 3. Contests--Fiction. 4. Veterans--Fiction. 5.
Afghan War, 2001---Fiction. 6. Colorado--Fiction.] I. Terrell, Brandon, 1978- author. II. Title.

  PZ7.M25643Sng 2015
  813.6--dc23

                                  2014022990

This book has been officially leveled by using the F&P Text Level Gradient™
Leveling System.

Art Director: Heather Kindseth
Designer: Veronica Scott
Production Specialist: Jennifer Walker

Photo Credits:
Shutterstock: Dudarev Mikhail, cover, Lizard, back cover, chapter openings, Yarygin, cover
(background)
Design Elements: Shutterstock

Printed in the United States of America in North Mankato, MN.
122014   008691R

TABLE OF CONTENTS

CHAPTER 1

HITTING THE SLOPES

"Come on, slowpoke! What's taking you so long?"

Kaleb Pearson crouched low on his snowboard and took off down the ski trail after his laughing stepbrother, Luke.

Luke was Kaleb's hero. At nineteen, Luke stood a foot taller than thirteen-year-old Kaleb. But their age difference had never changed their relationship. They were brothers and best friends.

Kaleb could still remember the first time he'd gone out riding with Luke and his stepfather, Nick. He'd been just six years old when they had first taken him to Ridgewood, a large ski resort just outside their hometown of Rock Springs, Colorado.

That first time he'd hit the slopes, his stepfather had strapped a pair of skis on a nervous Kaleb. "I don't think I can do this," Kaleb had said.

"Just keep your eyes on me," twelve-year-old Luke had said. He'd looked calm, standing on his own set of skis about twenty feet down the bunny hill from Kaleb. Luke had stretched out his arms. "You'll be fine, Kaleb. I'm right here."

Kaleb remembered letting go of Nick's hand, looking ahead to Luke, and gliding easily down the snowy hill. He remembered how exhilarating it had felt — the cool air striking his face and cheeks, his feet sliding easily underneath him.

He'd soon been wrapped up in his brother's arms. Off balance, the two boys had toppled to the ground, laughing hard at themselves for falling.

"See?" Luke had said. "I got you."

And he had. Always.

Now, on this cold but sunny April day, the two brothers were racing down Marvel Run, one of Ridgewood's back trails, on their snowboards. It wasn't a double black diamond — the most difficult of trails — but it was an intermediate.

In front of Kaleb, Luke carved to the left on his snowboard, heading toward a patch of berms, or ledges, in the snow. As he did, a wake of powdery fluff erupted behind him. The blast of snow hit Kaleb right in the face.

"Hey!" Kaleb shouted, wiping his goggles clear.

Luke laughed. Kaleb turned by shifting his weight onto the toeside of his board and followed Luke to the bumpy terrain. As he hit the first berm, Kaleb launched into the air. He extended his board in front of him and grabbed it with his front hand in a mute grab — a trick Luke had taught him. He landed solidly, his knees absorbing the impact.

Luke was far ahead of him but had turned back to watch Kaleb's run. "Sick mute!" he shouted.

"Thanks!" Kaleb replied.

As he boarded down the mountain, Kaleb thought back to the first time he and Luke had tried out their boards. They'd gotten them a few years back for Christmas, around the time Luke had graduated from downhill skiing and moved on to snowboarding. Kaleb, naturally, had followed.

Luke had tried to show him how to ride down the hill with his weight spread evenly on both feet and his board facing across the slope. He'd demonstrated on his new board, a vibrant red and blue deck with a white eagle on the bottom. The move had looked pretty simple.

"It's called sideslipping," Luke had explained.

Kaleb had scoffed. "Easy as pie," he'd replied confidently. He had then proceeded to faceplant and eat snow down the entire length of the hill.

But today, Kaleb raced down Marvel Run after his brother. Luke must have pulled back on his speed, because soon Kaleb was riding next to him.

These days, Luke and Kaleb didn't get out to Ridgewood much together. Luke lived on his own in Denver, about thirty miles away. He was also in the National Guard Reserve, which met every other weekend for training, so he had very little time to come visit. But the days Kaleb did spend with his stepbrother were some of the best he could ever recall.

Approaching the bottom of the run, Kaleb dug the heelside of his board into the snow until he came to a stop. Then he unstrapped his helmet and peeled the goggles off his windburned face.

"Not too shabby, little bro," Luke called out. He wiped the sweat off his forehead with the back of one gloved hand. "I'm gonna go for one more run. You in?"

"Nah, I'm gonna take a breather," Kaleb said. He sat in the snow and rested in the sunshine. He breathed in the cold air, feeling grateful for the time he got to spend with his big brother.

CHAPTER 2

STARTLING NEWS

"Hey, earth to Kaleb. Are you hungry?" Luke asked awhile later as he slid to a stop in front of Kaleb and pointed toward a chalet in the distance.

"I could use a little gas in the tank," Kaleb said, patting his stomach. He'd been daydreaming while Luke took another run.

Luke laughed. "Then lead the way, little man."

Kaleb and Luke unstrapped their back feet from the bindings of their boards. Then, pushing off with their free feet, they glided across the snow toward the chalet. It looked like a log cabin with smoke trailing out of a tall chimney on the roof.

The chalet's cafeteria was located in the building's lower level. Racks full of skis and snowboards were situated just outside a row of doors leading to the café and rental shop. Apparently Kaleb and Luke weren't the only people on the slopes today who needed to chow down.

Kaleb propped his deck — a yellow board with a black lightning bolt slashing across the bottom — in an empty spot on the rack. Luke leaned his next to Kaleb's.

From behind him, Kaleb heard a girl say, "Hey, Kaleb. What's up?"

Kaleb turned to see Amber, a girl from school, standing nearby. They had a few classes together, but they weren't really friends. Amber wore a red puffy jacket and white snowpants. Her hair was tucked inside a red stocking cap. On the left side of her coat, in white letters, were the words: JUNIOR SKI PATROL.

"Oh, hey, Amber," Kaleb said.

"Great day to board, isn't it?" Amber said, looking up at the cloudless sky.

Kaleb nodded. "Yeah."

"Hey," Luke interjected. "Aren't you going to introduce me to your friend, little bro?"

Kaleb nodded. "This is Amber," he said. "Amber, this is my annoying brother, Luke."

"By annoying, I think he means better at snowboarding and talking to girls and pretty much everything else," Luke said.

"Nice to meet you, Luke," Amber said with a smile, her face turning pink.

Girls always seemed to get flustered around Luke. Kaleb rolled his eyes. He hated to admit it, but it made him a little jealous.

"We're going inside to get something to eat," Luke said. "You wanna join us?"

Amber's face dropped. "Sorry, I can't. I have to check the back trails right now." She looked over at Kaleb. "Next time?"

Kaleb nodded. "Yeah. That'd be cool," he said, waving at Amber. Then he led the way into the building.

Once inside, Luke punched Kaleb on the arm with a soft thump. "She's cute, bro," he said.

Kaleb could feel his cheeks burning red with embarrassment. He pushed Luke back. "Knock it off."

The cafeteria was filled with people. Most had shed their oversized coats but still wore their snowpants and ski boots. They clunked around, some more gracefully than others. The air was heavy with the smell of hamburgers and French fries. Kaleb's stomach growled as he inhaled the mix of scents.

"Let's hurry," Kaleb said. "Before my stomach eats itself."

Kaleb and Luke hung their coats alongside all the others on the wall. Then they crossed the cafeteria, passing long tables and benches filled with people enjoying trays of food. One kid, his colorful stocking cap perched comically atop his head, recognized Luke and said hello.

There were numerous food choices — different kinds of pizza and sandwiches, warm soups, hot cocoa, a salad bar, and even a dessert station — but Kaleb had his mind set on a cheeseburger and fries. They found the correct line, grabbed a tray, and waited their turn.

When they'd found a spot to sit at one of the long tables, Luke said, "Kaleb, there's something I need to talk to you about."

Kaleb was suddenly nervous. Luke's tone of voice implied that whatever he was going to say, it was not going to be good news. Suddenly, the bite of cheeseburger Kaleb was chewing lost all flavor, and he swallowed nervously. "Yeah? What's up?" he asked.

Luke paused, taking a moment to gaze out the large bay window that framed Ridgewood's widest trail, the Mother Lode. Then he said, "I'm being deployed."

"What?" Kaleb dropped his cheeseburger onto his tray. "What do you mean?"

"My National Guard unit is being sent overseas soon. I guess they need the backup," Luke replied.

"When?" The pitch of Kaleb's voice had gone up a notch. It cracked as he spoke.

"One month — the second week of May," Luke said. "We head to Georgia for training and then over to the Middle East."

"Where? Where in the Middle East?" Kaleb asked.

Luke shrugged. "I don't know yet."

"How long will you be gone?" Though he tried to remain calm, panic had begun to creep into Kaleb's words.

Luke noticed, and in his usual calm tone, said, "Hey, little bro. Take it easy." It was the same calmness that had eased Kaleb's nerves the first time he'd skied, all those years ago. "I'll be gone for about a year — "

"A year!" Kaleb shouted. Some of the people around them started to stare.

Luke looked into Kaleb's eyes and said quietly, "A year. But hey, I'm going to be just fine, okay?"

Kaleb's hands shook, and his heart banged hard against his ribcage. He took a deep breath to calm his nerves. It helped, but only a little.

"Now eat up," Luke said. "We've got some more boarding to do before it gets dark."

"Yeah, okay," Kaleb mumbled. He ate a handful of bland fries and washed them down with tasteless soda.

When the brothers were finished eating, they gathered up their garbage and trays. As they walked outside Luke repeated, "Kaleb, I'm going to be just fine."

And because Luke was Kaleb's hero, Kaleb believed him.

CHAPTER 3

TIME MARCHES ON

As the summer passed, Kaleb spoke with his brother often. Even though Luke was in Georgia for training, the brothers had exchanged emails pretty much every day. But in mid-July, Luke had been sent to a small city in northern Afghanistan.

Since then, Kaleb's chances to speak with his big brother had become more rare. When they could, he and Luke would find time to video chat over the computer.

Kaleb had found very little time to snowboard recently between the school year starting and helping his stepdad at the antique shop he owned in Rock Springs. The shop specialized in old musical instruments and rare books. Even though he was only thirteen, Kaleb watched the register when his stepdad needed to help customers.

When he did make it out to Ridgewood, Kaleb often found himself hanging out with Amber. They carved down Ridgewood's trails together, Kaleb on his snowboard and Amber on her skis. Now that school had begun again, he and Amber often ate lunch together and sometimes hung out after school.

One night in October, Kaleb and Luke had scheduled a time to video chat. Kaleb logged in, clicked the "call" button, and waited for the fuzzy image of his brother to pop up on the computer screen. Luke's head finally filled the frame.

"Hey!" Kaleb said, louder than necessary.

"Hi, little brother! Anything new I should know about?" Luke asked.

"Nope. School. Snowboard. Sleep. Repeat," Kaleb said. "You?"

"Nothing but sand out here," Luke reported. "I miss the cold and the snow. Can't wait to strap on a snowboard. Some of the guys and I tried to board down a sand dune last week."

"Ha! How'd you do?" Kaleb asked.

"Not good, man. I'll email you the video after we hang up," Luke said.

Luke and Kaleb talked for over an hour, catching up and laughing. Kaleb was sad to say goodbye, but sure enough, when he checked his email later that night, there was a message from Luke. In the video, three men in camouflage pants and tan T-shirts ran up a hill.

Kaleb recognized Luke on the left. He seemed taller and stronger than he'd been when he left. Luke carried a long, flat piece of metal, which he placed on the sand and stood on top of. The two other men gave him a push, and Luke took off down the hill. He made it halfway before he flipped over, and his face landed right in the sand.

Kaleb laughed until his sides hurt. He probably watched the video a dozen times the night Luke sent it to him.

And that was how things went for a while. Emails. An occasional letter in the mail. A video chat here and there.

Sure, one year felt like an eternity, but it looked like things were going to be all right.

* * *

The day Kaleb's world changed, it was cold and threatening to snow. Winter had not quite arrived, but it was letting everyone know that it was on its way.

Kaleb biked home from school, the crisp wind biting into every inch of his exposed skin. He had stupidly left his gloves and hat at home.

When he rounded the corner onto his street, hopping his bike up onto the empty sidewalk,

Kaleb saw his stepdad's battered red Jeep parked in the driveway.

That's weird, he thought. *Nick should be at the shop for another couple of hours.*

Kaleb rode up the driveway and ditched his bike near the garage. Two steps inside the door, Kaleb could hear his mother crying in the living room. It wasn't a wailing cry, but a sniffling, soft hitch of breath.

Kaleb's thoughts went immediately to his brother. Instinctively, he knew that something had happened to Luke.

Kaleb hurried into the living room and saw his mom and stepdad sitting together on the couch. Kaleb's mom had her face buried in her hands, and Nick's arm was draped over her shoulder. Though he wasn't crying, Nick's eyes were bloodshot. When he saw Kaleb, he fought back a fresh wave of tears.

"What's wrong?" Kaleb asked.

Kaleb's mom jerked, startled by the sound of his voice. She clearly hadn't heard him come in the house. Still, she didn't look up.

"Hey, pal," Nick said in a quiet voice. "Sit down for a second."

"No," Kaleb said. "What happened? Is it Luke? Is he okay?" Then, more to himself than to his parents, he added, "Oh man, please let him be okay."

"Luke's gonna be all right," Nick explained. "He's alive."

A flood of relief washed over Kaleb, but he was still confused by his parents' grief. "Then what is it?" he asked.

"Luke's unit was driving from one city to another," Nick explained. "Their truck ran over an IED — a type of bomb — and it blew up."

Retelling the news sent Kaleb's mom into a fresh wave of tears. Nick squeezed her, trying to be strong despite the situation.

"A few of the guys were seriously hurt, but it seems Luke took it the worst," Nick continued. "The doctors had to . . . to . . ." He choked up a bit but then swallowed down his grief. "They had to amputate his left leg below the knee," he finished.

"Amputate?" Kaleb repeated. He felt like somebody had punched him in the stomach. He thought of Luke, out there in the sand, hurt and alone. He'd lost a leg. It was nearly too much to take.

All of the things we do together. Run. Play basketball. Snowboard out at Ridgewood. Nothing will ever be the same again, Kaleb thought.

It was with this thought that the tears finally came.

CHAPTER 4

FALLEN HERO

The next day, Kaleb and his mom sat in the waiting room at Veteran's Medical Hospital, a large stone building in downtown Denver. Luke's flight had landed earlier that morning. Nick had gone to Denver International Airport to meet the military plane and was riding to the hospital in the ambulance with Luke.

The waiting area was carpeted, with large chairs and a couple of couches beside tables stacked with magazines. A television played a college basketball game on low volume, and a row of computers lined one wall.

Kaleb's mom checked her watch for the millionth time and then nervously wrung her hands together. "They should be here any minute," she said.

Kaleb stood and stretched his legs. "We've been sitting here for almost two hours," he said, walking over to a vending machine. He dug out a couple of one-dollar bills from his pocket and bought himself a bottle of soda.

"The last time Nick called, he said an ambulance would be bringing them over from the airport shortly," Kaleb's mom said.

A few minutes later, while Kaleb was sipping his soda and zoning out watching basketball, his mom's phone beeped with a text message. "They're here," she said. "They'll be bringing Luke to room 3603."

With that, she stood and slid the phone into her enormous purse. Kaleb followed her out into the hallway where a receptionist in blue scrubs directed them to the elevators. They headed up to the third floor and wove through the maze of hallways until they finally arrived at the 3600 wing.

"Grace! Kaleb!" Nick shouted down the hall.

Kaleb turned to see a gurney being pushed by three nurses headed toward them. Nick walked along beside it.

"Oh, Nick," Kaleb's mom said. She hurried over and wrapped Nick in a big hug.

Kaleb followed, but his eyes never left the gurney. Lying there, covered by blankets and fast asleep, was Luke. There were thin scratches on his face and a bandage on his forehead. Dark circles made his eyes look old and tired. Kaleb didn't dare look down at Luke's legs.

"They gave him a sedative. It'll help him sleep, so he won't be in so much pain," Nick explained. He placed his hands on Kaleb's shoulders to comfort him.

They all continued down the hall until they reached Luke's room. The nurses worked quickly to get Luke settled, and soon, Kaleb's family was alone.

"His doctors will be coming to visit soon," Nick said, "as well as a prosthetist and physical therapist. They say it's best to start getting him moving around as soon as possible."

"That's great," Kaleb's mom said. "They'll take very good care of him here."

"What's a prosthetist?" Kaleb asked.

"Someone who'll measure him for a new leg," Nick said.

"So he'll walk again?" Kaleb asked.

Nick nodded. "It will take a lot of work, but that's the plan."

Kaleb looked over at Luke, who was still sleeping peacefully. He looked fragile. Kaleb's eyes drifted down to the blankets covering Luke's legs. Beneath the crisp linens, Kaleb could see the outline of Luke's right leg, long and lean, ending with the peak of his foot jutting upward. Next to it, though, where the matching peak should rise, there was nothing. The sheets and blankets were flat up to Luke's knee.

"I think he's waking up," Kaleb's mom said quietly.

Kaleb looked back up at Luke's face and saw his brother's eyes flutter open and shut. Finally he managed to keep them open.

"Hey, little brother," Luke said through dry and cracked lips. His words were like sand skittering across paper.

"Hey, Luke," Kaleb said. Tears welled up in his eyes, but he quickly brushed them away.

Luke reached out with one bandaged hand. A number of tubes wound from under his bandages to an IV hanger with bags of fluids.

Kaleb took his brother's hand in his and squeezed it tight. "Welcome home," he whispered.

CHAPTER 5

RECKLESS

Later that afternoon, Kaleb rode the city bus to Ridgewood. He needed to vent, and snowboarding was the best way to do it. He pulled his phone out from his jacket pocket and thought about texting Amber to see if she wanted to meet up. *But I could really use some time alone,* he thought, shoving the phone back in his pocket.

Kaleb wore earbuds and was listening to music at a blistering volume. His board was tucked between his legs, and he clutched his helmet in his hands. He couldn't stop thinking about Luke lying in his hospital bed, wrapped in bandages.

It isn't fair, Kaleb thought, twisting the strap of his helmet around his fingers in anger. *Luke doesn't deserve this at all.*

When he reached the ski resort, he showed his lift pass to the guy at the entrance and went straight for the nearest chairlift. As he crossed the hard-packed snow, his board still tucked under his arm, Amber came riding past him on skis.

"Hi, Kaleb!" she said cheerily.

Kaleb still had his earbuds in under his hat and barely heard her over the loud music. He didn't want to talk to anyone anyway. He just wanted to board. So Kaleb just nodded and went on his way.

The chairlift took him to a few of the easier trails on the front side of the mountain. Kaleb made his way down a trail called the Mother Lode. He tried to gain as much speed as possible, launching into 360 and 540 spins when he could.

The slopes were busy that afternoon, and Kaleb had to weave his way past skiers and snowboarders on every trail. They were cautious, enjoying themselves and in no hurry to reach the bottom. To Kaleb, everyone looked like they were moving in slow motion. He sped down recklessly, not caring if he fell, almost hoping he did.

On his second pass down Streamline, an easy trail, Kaleb nearly ran into an older gentleman helping a young girl down the hill. The little girl had her skis crossed in front of her in a snowplow maneuver, and the older man held her hand. Kaleb saw them at the last second and swerved to avoid them. He missed hitting the man by inches.

"Hey!" the man shouted furiously. "Slow down, and watch where you're going!"

Yeah, right, Kaleb thought. Instead, he made his way to the backside of the mountain, where the more advanced trails were located.

Kaleb stopped at the top of the Recluse, a double black diamond trail. The run was flanked on both sides by tree trunks and an occasional evergreen or outcropping of rock. Kaleb and Luke had often joked about racing down the Recluse, but neither had ever tried the trail.

That changes today, Kaleb thought. He stared down at the winding and steep trail. Then he twisted his board, leaned forward, and began his descent.

At first, the trail seemed pretty easy. Kaleb hit the turns perfectly and even found a spot to get a little air. But then the trail narrowed, and the curving slope became treacherous. Kaleb rocketed down the hill, barely missing a large boulder that jutted out of the snow and split the trail in two. His tail clipped the rock, throwing him off balance.

Kaleb tried to regain his stability just as the Recluse banked hard to the left. He dug in on his toeside and leaned low in an extreme carve. His face was a foot from the snow, his gloved hand skimming the trail's bumpy surface. But he couldn't hold on.

Kaleb's board stuck, and suddenly he was airborne. He hit the snow hard, and the impact knocked the air out of his lungs. His feet unlatched from his board's bindings. Thankfully, he was wearing a helmet, because when he fell, the back of his head struck the hard ground, and he saw stars.

Kaleb groaned and looked around. His head was feet from the thick, gray trunk of a tree. His board was downhill, stopped next to an evergreen.

Kaleb lay on his back in the snow for some time, alone. No other skiers or snowboarders ventured down the Recluse. Every muscle in Kaleb's body ached. His right ankle throbbed. *I must have twisted it in the straps,* he thought.

Carefully, Kaleb rose to his feet. He put some weight on his right ankle and felt pinpricks of pain. He grimaced. Luckily, he could still walk on it. He carefully waddled to his board, taking small steps to make sure he didn't injure his ankle any more than it already was.

"Oh, man," Kaleb muttered as he picked up his snowboard. The tail of it had cracked, and there were large scratches along the bottom.

Kaleb sat in the snow for a while, catching his breath. *What am I doing?* he thought. *I could have hit that tree head-on. Or seriously injured my ankle. If I'm not careful, I'll wind up in the hospital, too.*

Kaleb looked up and saw a person skiing down the slope toward him. As the skier neared, he recognized her bright red jacket and white snowpants. Amber came to a stop next to him. "Hey," she said.

"Hey," he mumbled back.

"So . . . you're not going to avoid me now?" she asked.

"Sorry about that," Kaleb replied sheepishly.

"You okay?" Amber asked. She nodded toward his board and leaned forward on her ski poles.

"No." Kaleb shook his head. "No, I'm not."

Like a tidal wave, the whole story came pouring out of him. He told Amber about Luke's injury. About seeing him in the hospital. About coming out to Ridgewood and not caring if he hurt himself. He didn't cry, but he knew that Amber wouldn't care if he had.

Finally, after Kaleb had spilled his guts, Amber said, "I'm really, really sorry Kaleb! I know how much Luke means to you."

"Yeah," Kaleb said. "He's my hero. And now he's . . ." He trailed off.

"If you need to talk to someone," Amber said, "I'm right here. But be safe, okay?"

Kaleb nodded. Then he watched as Amber cautiously began to ski down the Recluse.

Kaleb scooped up his broken board and began to limp down the hill after her, careful not to put too much weight on his bad ankle. *I'm lucky it wasn't worse,* Kaleb thought.

CHAPTER 6

A HELPING HAND

After his near-disaster out at Ridgewood, Kaleb decided to take a break from snowboarding — both to clear his mind and rest his hurt ankle — for the next month.

Snowboarding conditions weren't great this time of year anyway. December always brought rough winds and cold fronts that made spending more than a few minutes out on the mountains miserable. And since Kaleb's board had been busted up in his accident, too, he'd need to get a new one before hitting the slopes again.

Besides, Kaleb wanted to spend as much time as possible with Luke as he healed from his injury and began rehab. Kaleb spent most of his afternoons at the hospital. Nights, too, if he didn't have school the next day. He'd pull the uncomfortable leather armchair out into a makeshift cot and watch TV or do homework as he lay next to Luke.

Luke didn't talk much these days. Kaleb figured it was good just to be by his side, though, so he also accompanied Luke to almost all of his physical therapy sessions at the hospital's state-of-the-art facility for rehabilitation. Three times a day, Luke's physical therapist, Hugh, would help him into a wheelchair, and they would spend an hour working on his upper-body strength.

For the most part, Luke kept his legs hidden under blankets when Kaleb was around. That was okay. Kaleb wasn't sure he was ready to see the extent of Luke's injuries.

One evening after Kaleb finished helping Nick over at the antique shop, he hitched a ride on the city bus to the hospital. The halls of the third floor smelled like food, and Kaleb's stomach rumbled. He hadn't eaten dinner yet.

When he reached Luke's room, Kaleb found his brother propped up in bed. In his lap sat a metal artificial leg.

"Hey," Kaleb said. "Are they finally ready to let you try it out?"

"Soon," Luke said.

"Can I see?" Kaleb asked.

"Sure." Luke placed the metal appendage in Kaleb's hands.

"Whoa. It's really lightweight," Kaleb said.

"Yeah, it's made out of carbon fiber," Luke explained.

Kaleb looked closely at the prosthetic. At one end was a cupped area lined with foam. "So that's where your knee will go?"

Luke nodded. "The socket. They measured me to make sure it'll be a perfect fit."

From the socket, there was a long rod that ended in a metal piece that simulated a foot. It bent and turned.

After examining the prosthetic, Kaleb placed it on a counter and returned to his usual spot in the armchair. A rolling side table next to Luke's bed held a covered tray of food. Kaleb lifted the lid to find a half-eaten grilled cheese sandwich and an apple. "You gonna eat those?" he asked.

Luke shook his head. "Have at them."

Kaleb devoured the food. As he ate, he snatched the remote — attached to a cord next to Luke's bed — and flipped on the television. They watched a bit of some dumb sitcom without saying a word. It was just nice to be in each other's company.

Around the time that visiting hours were over, Luke's regular nurse, Nurse Franklin, entered

Luke's room. Tucked under one arm was a pillow. She handed it to Kaleb and said, "Sticking around again tonight?"

Kaleb nodded. "Yeah. My parents said it was okay."

"I'll make sure you both get a good breakfast then," Nurse Franklin said. "Our little secret." She winked on her way out the door.

Kaleb mindlessly changed channels until he happened to come across an extreme snowboarding competition on the sports channel. One of the competitors had just finished his run on the halfpipe, and they were showing the highlights in slow motion.

"Check it out," Kaleb said, nudging Luke, who was drifting in and out of sleep.

Luke stirred just as the TV showed a replay of the boarder executing a double McTwist 1260. Flashes popped and snapped from surrounding cameras as the athlete turned fluidly on his board.

"That is so amazing," Kaleb said. He crunched down on the apple. Juice ran down his chin, and he wiped it off with the sleeve of his hoodie. "Luke? Did you see that?"

"Turn it off," Luke said quietly. His mood had shifted. He was annoyed now.

"What?" Kaleb asked, pointing at the TV. "Seriously bro, did you see that? The dude's a snowboarding god."

"I said turn it off, Kaleb." Luke's words were sharp, edged with anger.

"Why?" Kaleb asked.

"Just do it." Luke turned to his side, away from Kaleb. He pulled the sheets up closer around him. "I don't want to see anything about snowboarding," he said.

"Oh." Kaleb clicked off the TV, and the room was silent.

"It's just another stupid reminder of what I can't do anymore," Luke said bitterly.

Kaleb hadn't meant to hurt Luke's feelings. Before the accident, they'd spend hours watching snowboarding competitions together. He'd just assumed Luke would still want to do that.

"Sorry," Kaleb said quietly.

His brother didn't respond. Whether Luke heard him or he had already fallen asleep, Kaleb couldn't tell.

After a moment, Kaleb lay back in the chair-turned-cot, closed his eyes, and tried to shut out the hospital sounds as best he could.

CHAPTER 7

X-TREME COMPETE

As winter break and the holidays passed by, Kaleb started getting the snowboarding itch again. He just had to get back out on the slopes.

The Saturday after Christmas, Kaleb woke up energized. *Today's the day,* he thought. *Now I just have to find a board to use . . .*

Kaleb's snowboard was still broken from when he'd tried to board down the Recluse last month. But as he lay there in bed, Kaleb remembered that Luke might have his snowboard tucked away somewhere in his old room.

Kaleb texted Amber to see if she'd be at Ridgewood and then headed to the kitchen to ask his stepdad for a ride. After a quick meal of cereal and OJ, Kaleb rushed to his room to get ready.

"Hurry up if you want a lift to the slopes, kiddo!" Nick called from the hallway. "I've gotta stop by work before heading to the hospital!"

"Just a second!" Kaleb shouted back. He hurried over to Luke's old bedroom.

Before being deployed, Luke had moved out of his apartment and back into the family home. The room was mostly just stacks of boxes, though, now more of a storage unit than a bedroom. It was weird being in Luke's room. The walls were still the brilliant shade of blue Luke had painted them one weekend when their parents had been away. A few posters of sports stars hung around the room.

Kaleb made his way toward the closet. He pulled open the door and spotted the snowboard right away. The red and blue board with a white eagle on it was hidden in the corner underneath some clothes. Kaleb dug it out, held it up, and turned it around in his hands.

Perfect. I can't wait to show this to Amber today, he thought.

Just then, Nick's car horn honked outside, and Kaleb dashed out of Luke's room, snowboard in hand, closing the door behind him.

* * *

"Wow. I wonder what's going on here," Kaleb's stepdad said as they pulled into the parking lot at Ridgewood.

Much of the huge lot was filled with long, wide semitrucks. They were coated in dirt and dust from the highways, but underneath the grime, most were vibrant and colorful and had logos that read: X-TREME COMPETE! Men and women worked to unload equipment from the backs of some trucks.

"X-treme Compete is here?" Kaleb said. He was confused but excited. The company set up snowboard competitions all over the world. He needed to find Amber right away.

Nick pulled up to the chalet and said, "I'll be back to pick you up this afternoon."

Kaleb shouted goodbye and slammed the Jeep door closed. With Luke's board tucked under his arm, he dashed — as well as he could in snowboard boots — into the chalet to show his slope pass and then headed toward the chairlifts.

He found Amber at the bottom of the Mother Lode. She was on her skis, offering directions to a couple of the X-treme Compete guys.

"Welcome to the chaos, Kaleb," she said when she saw him.

"What's going on?" Kaleb asked. He looked up at the Mother Lode. The wide trail had been mostly closed off to skiers and boarders. A bright orange temporary fence surrounded it.

"Yeah, you haven't been here in a while," Amber said. "X-treme Compete paid to transform one of our slopes for a slopestyle snowboarding competition in a few weeks."

"Slopestyle?" Kaleb said. "Really?" He had heard of slopestyle before. It was a downhill competition in which boarders performed aerial tricks as well as tricks on boxes and rails. Slopestyle had been around for a while and was one of the most popular events at the X-Games. It was gaining popularity as a regular event in the Winter Olympics, too.

"They're setting up the course right there on the Mother Lode," Amber explained, pointing to the closed trail.

"So there's going to be a bunch of professional snowboarders coming here?" Kaleb asked.

Amber nodded. "Yep. They're even going to have a local amateur competition. Twenty-five boarders can enter. It's a day before the pros compete." She smiled at him and added, "You know, if you're interested."

Kaleb shook his head. "Nah, I couldn't," he said. "But man, it'd be cool."

"Think about it," Amber said. She pointed to his snowboard. "Hey, new board?"

"Yeah. It's Luke's, actually," Kaleb explained. "I busted mine up last time I was here."

"Oh, right. When you nearly killed yourself on the Recluse," Amber said.

Kaleb shook his head and gave her a slight smile. He tried not to think about that run and how impulsive he'd been that day. He really could have wound up in a hospital bed next to Luke if he hadn't been so lucky.

"Hey, my lunch break is at one o'clock today," Amber said. "You wanna meet me in the cafeteria?"

Kaleb smiled. "Yeah," he said. "Yeah, that'd be cool," he said.

"Cool. See you then," Amber said before walking away.

Kaleb strapped his front foot onto his board, pushed off with his back foot, and glided across the snow toward the nearest chairlift.

As the lift carried him up to the midpoint of the mountain, where many of the trails connected, Kaleb looked down at the Mother Lode. Soon it would be filled with rail boxes and enormous jumps.

I bet camera crews will be filming from all over, he thought. *Probably even from somewhere on this lift.* Kaleb was pumped to get to witness such a big event in the snowboarding world.

Luke would have killed it in slopestyle, Kaleb thought. *But I'd never have the courage to board down that course.*

Kaleb wished he could tell Luke about the event, but after his brother's reaction to the competition on TV, there was no way he was going to bring up snowboarding again.

CHAPTER 8

STRUGGLING

That evening, Kaleb went with his parents to visit Luke. When they reached Luke's room, they found it empty except for Nurse Franklin. "Hugh just took him to physical therapy with his new prosthetic," she told them.

"Thank you," Kaleb's mom said, shrugging off her coat. "We'll just wait here for him."

Kaleb hadn't seen Luke wearing his prosthetic leg yet and really wanted to check it out. "Can I go watch him?" he asked the nurse.

"Of course," she answered.

t his mom for confirmation, he took the elevator down to , where the physical therapy room ated. As he walked toward the open door, Kaleb spied Luke and his therapist by a set of long parallel bars and was struck by the sight of Luke standing without his crutches. With the prosthetic leg attached to his, Luke stood between the bars, holding on with both hands. He wore a pair of new running shoes that were so white they practically glowed.

Hugh, Luke's physical therapist, was a stout man in his midthirties with a receding hairline and a scruffy, unshaven face. He saw Kaleb from across the room and recognized him. "Looks like we have some company, Luke," he said.

Luke turned to look over his shoulder. "Hey," he said without a shred of excitement.

"We were just getting started," Hugh said, motioning for Kaleb to join them. Kaleb walked over and sat down on the floor near the bars as Hugh continued. "We're done with all of those sitting exercises, Luke. Our focus now is to regain your center of gravity. Okay?"

Luke nodded.

"The idea is to get your body moving while teaching your brain to balance again," Hugh said. "How's the pressure on your prosthetic?"

"So-so," Luke said with a grimace.

"Let's see you walk," Hugh said, folding his arms across his chest and taking a step back.

Luke hesitated for a moment, still clutching the bars. Then he took a step forward with his artificial leg. The move looked awkward and clumsy, almost robotic. Kaleb thought of his brother running up the sand dune in his video, and his heart hurt.

Luke stepped forward with his real leg, and his balance shifted. He gripped the bars tighter. Determination set in, and Luke began to shuffle forward. He was getting the hang of it.

"Great job, Luke," Kaleb whispered, afraid he'd break Luke's concentration if he spoke louder.

About three-quarters of the way down the bars, Luke let go and balanced on his own.

"Are you sure?" Hugh asked, stepping forward.

Luke waved him off. He took another step and tried to center his weight but lost his balance. As he fell, Luke grabbed at the bars. He missed. With a giant thud, he landed face-first on the mat. Luke yelled and angrily pounded his fists on the mat like a child having a tantrum.

Kaleb crouched beside his brother. "Here," he said, "let me help you —"

"Leave me alone!" Luke shouted. He cursed under his breath.

Hugh, calm and collected, said, "Let's call it a night. You've done some great work today, Luke."

Kaleb retreated from the physical therapy room. Luke had never yelled at him before, and it hurt more than he ever thought it could.

* * *

As he lay in bed that night, Kaleb thought about Luke. *There must be something I can do to help,* Kaleb thought. *I hate seeing Luke depressed.*

Luke was like a different person lately. It seemed to Kaleb that his brother had forgotten what it was like to be happy. There had to be a way to cheer him up and put the fight back into him.

I wish I could show him all of the things he taught me, Kaleb thought. *Like bravery. And confidence. And facing your fears . . . that's it!*

Kaleb reached over to his dresser and grabbed his phone. Amber's name was at the top of his contacts. She answered right away.

"Is there still room on the list for the amateur slopestyle competition?" Kaleb asked.

"Dunno," she said. "I'm going over to Ridgewood in the morning, though. Do you want me to try to sign you up?"

"Definitely," Kaleb said without hesitation.

CHAPTER 9

SLOPESTYLE

As he ate breakfast with his stepdad the next morning, Kaleb stared at his phone resting on the table. While he waited for Amber to call, he started to tell Nick about the X-treme Compete event.

But suddenly, Kaleb's phone began to buzz.

"Ull-oh?" he mumbled, quickly chewing and swallowing a mouthful of sugary cereal.

"Kaleb?" Amber asked. She sounded confused.

"Yeah. Yeah, it's me. Sorry. Eating," Kaleb said.

"I checked. There's one slot left," Amber said. "And it's all yours if you want it."

"Yes!" Kaleb was so excited he leaped to his feet, bumping the table and sloshing soggy cereal and milk over the edge of his bowl.

"The course is open today so boarders can practice," Amber said. "Do you want me to show you around? My shift ends at two o'clock."

"That'd be great!" Kaleb replied. His plan was coming together perfectly.

* * *

That afternoon, though, Kaleb was unsure. *What was I thinking?* he asked himself as he stood beside Amber at the top of the course. He looked down, and the rush of adrenaline he'd felt upon finding out he was entered in the competition fizzled. It was the most intimidating thing he'd ever seen. Several ski patrollers were monitoring the area to make sure no one got injured.

"It reminds me of a skate park," Kaleb said.

"That was an inspiration for slopestyle," Amber said. "Do you skateboard?"

Kaleb nodded. "Yeah, a little bit. Luke used to take me to a pretty sweet skate park in Denver."

"Cool," Amber said. "We should try it out sometime. So . . . are you ready?"

Kaleb swallowed the knot that was growing in his throat. "Why not?" he replied.

He lined up at the top of the run. It was only the second time he'd boarded since his accident the previous month, when he'd injured not just his ankle and his board but also his pride.

Kaleb slid his goggles down over his eyes. "Wish me luck," he said.

"Luck," Amber said. "I'll follow you down. See you at the bottom."

Kaleb hesitated. *I wonder if I'm being just as reckless as I was on the Recluse,* he thought. *What if I hurt my ankle again?* But then Kaleb thought of Luke's bravery and remembered why he'd decided to do this. He needed to take chances and show courage for Luke . . . like Luke had done for him all these years. He turned his board — Luke's board — and shoved off.

On his first run, Kaleb just wanted to get a feel for the course, maybe try hitting a rail or two. The first jumps were smooth. He got a bit of air and landed perfectly. His knees and ankles absorbed each impact easily.

Immediately after each jump was a set of long, wide boxes flanking a rail. As Kaleb approached the next jump, he kept his board straight and ollied into a 50-50 slide, gliding along the railing.

The last rail met up with the spot where the Mother Lode evened off. His confidence returning, Kaleb looked past the level ground. The X-treme Compete people had added two big jumps to the course. They were so large that Kaleb couldn't even see the bottom of the trail from where he was.

Kaleb hit the first jump and though he didn't get a ton of air, he was still surprised at how high he flew. His landing was wobbly, and he nearly wiped out. He held on, got his bearings, and hit the second jump at maximum speed.

For a moment, Kaleb felt weightless, like he could touch the clouds. Then gravity pulled him down, and he spread his arms for balance. His board hit the snow, and he turned, braking right away. Both hands skittered across the snow and helped steady him. When he came to a stop, he was still upright. And beyond exhilarated.

Amber was right behind him. She came to a stop about five feet away and peeled up her goggles. "Wow!" she shouted. "That was amazing!"

"I can't believe I did that!" Kaleb said, laughing. For a split second, he'd forgotten about Luke, about sleepless nights, and about worrying that his brother would never be the same.

"You'd better believe it, because we're about to do it again," Amber said, already skiing toward the chairlift. "You coming or what?"

"You know it!" Kaleb said, taking off after her.

CHAPTER 10

THE BIG DAY

Over the next few weeks, Kaleb spent as many hours as he could practicing on the slopestyle course. He and Amber would head to Ridgewood on the city bus after school each day to practice. As he got more comfortable, Kaleb had started to incorporate a few moves into his jumps.

Kaleb really wanted to tell Luke about the competition. But he was afraid that if his brother found out before the big day, he'd refuse to come to Ridgewood to watch. So Kaleb kept quiet about it and made sure his parents did, too.

The week before the competition, Kaleb and Amber spent all day on Saturday practicing at Ridgewood. Amber had been a great support system for Kaleb, and she gave him a lot of pointers about his technique on jumps and tricks. Although she was a skier, she knew a thing or two about snowboarding from working and watching countless competitions while on ski patrol at the resort.

As Kaleb rounded a corner near the end of the run, he saw Amber in her red jacket waiting for him. "Way to go, Kaleb! I think that was your best run yet!" she shouted as he slowed to a stop beside her.

Kaleb was starting to feel more confident, but he knew he'd have to be on top of his game next week at the competition.

* * *

The night before the event, Kaleb couldn't sleep. His insides felt twisted up like pretzels, and his heart was racing. Every time he closed his eyes, all he did was visualize the course. He planned out every move, every jump. He envisioned himself taking the last, long, gigantic leap into the sky, landing at the bottom, and seeing the smile on Luke's face. In his daydream, though, Luke was standing on his own, with both of his legs.

Around six in the morning, Kaleb heard his parents clanging around in the kitchen. He got up, took a quick shower, and slid into a pair of long johns, a hooded sweatshirt, and a pair of snowpants.

"Morning, bud," Nick said as Kaleb walked into the kitchen. "I'm making some tea. You want a mug?"

Kaleb shrugged. "Sure." He liked that Nick treated him more like a grown-up than a kid.

They sat together in silence, sipping tea and reading the newspaper, until Kaleb's mom joined them. She wore a bathrobe, and her hair was frizzy on one side. "Ready for your big day?" she asked as she hugged Kaleb around the neck.

"Absolutely," he answered. And he was.

After a simple breakfast of scrambled eggs and toast, Kaleb and his parents drove to pick up Luke at the hospital.

He was going to be released the following week, but he had been given a temporary leave for the day. Nick had told him they were going to have a family outing.

Luke and Hugh were waiting for them outside the front doors to the hospital. Luke sat in a wheelchair with a blanket draped over his legs. Hugh leaned against a set of crutches. Both wore large, puffy coats.

"Bringing the wheelchair?" Nick asked casually as he got out of the car to help Luke.

Luke didn't answer the question. Instead, he asked one of his own. "Where are we going?"

"It's a surprise," Kaleb told him.

Luke's scrunched-up expression made it clear he wasn't happy to hear this bit of news.

Nick and Hugh carefully helped Luke into the passenger's seat, folded the wheelchair up, and stored it in the back beside Kaleb's snowboard, which was tucked out of sight. Hugh waved as they drove off.

The car ride was quiet, with just the sound of the radio softly playing. Luke sat silently, staring out the window . . . until he realized where they were headed. "Why are we going to Ridgewood?" he asked in clipped words.

"I'm competing in a slopestyle competition today," Kaleb said nervously from the backseat. "And I want you to be there."

Luke began to protest, then simply grunted and went back to staring out the window.

Kaleb had never seen the parking lot at Ridgewood so packed. Every spot was filled. Television trucks and vans were set up near the chalet. Satellite dishes sprang from the news vehicles' roofs.

Nick drove right up the chalet to let them out before parking. He walked around to the passenger's side to help Luke out of the car. "You want the crutches?" he asked.

Luke shook his head, so Nick pulled the wheelchair out of the back and helped Luke into it.

Kaleb's mom pushed the chair toward the throng of people standing outside the chalet. Kaleb walked alongside, carrying Luke's old snowboard. If Luke noticed the board, he didn't say anything.

Kaleb dialed Amber on his phone. "We're here," he said, speaking loudly over the music pumping from nearby speakers.

"I'm by the judge's booth," she answered, just as loudly. "Do you see me?"

Kaleb craned his neck, looking around. He spotted the judge's booth at the base of the course. It was a long podium surrounded by flat-screen monitors, which gave the judges various camera angles of the course. There, in her bright red coat, waving her arms wildly over her head, was Amber.

"Go on ahead," Kaleb's mom said, tapping Kaleb on the shoulder. "We'll track Nick down and then find ourselves a good spot to watch. Good luck, honey." She squeezed him in a tight hug.

Kaleb hesitated, waiting for Luke to add something, but nothing came. It hurt his feelings that he didn't seem to have his brother's support, but he couldn't focus on it.

As he began to walk toward Amber, a guy with spiky blond hair, sunglasses, and an X-treme Compete jacket stopped him. "Hey, man, what's your name?" the guy asked. He was carrying a clipboard and clearly working the event.

"Kaleb Pearson."

The man checked his clipboard, nodded, and crossed something off his list. "All right. Hang tight. Lineup starts in fifteen minutes."

Kaleb waited nervously among the boarders while Amber was called away for ski-patrol duties. "Good luck," she said, giving him a quick hug.

"Thanks," Kaleb replied.

Finally, the music died down, and a woman bundled in bright X-treme Compete gear climbed up on the judge's stand. "Hi, everyone!" she announced. "Welcome to the X-treme Compete Amateur Slopestyle Competition!" The crowd hooted and hollered. "Will today's contestants please join me on stage?" the woman continued.

Kaleb and the others climbed a set of stairs leading onto the podium and lined up next to one another. He searched the crowd for his family and found them toward the front. His parents waved, but Luke did not.

The emcee made her way down the line, holding out the microphone to each competitor. One by one, the contestants offered their names and some information about themselves.

When she reached Kaleb, he quietly spoke into the mic. "My name is Kaleb Pearson," he said.

"And what made you join the competition today, Kaleb?" the emcee asked.

Kaleb cleared his throat. "Um, well, the reason I'm competing today is my brother, Luke."

He paused and looked at Luke, who seemed startled by mention of his name. "I never would have had the courage to compete today if it wasn't for him. Partly because he's the one who taught me how to snowboard. But mostly because he's always shown me the true meaning of bravery and strength. He is — and always will be — my hero."

The crowd broke into a round of applause. A few people whistled and cheered. Kaleb beamed with pride. He looked down at his family, and though he couldn't be sure, he thought he saw a hint of a smile creeping across Luke's lips and tears in his eyes.

CHAPTER 11

NAILING IT

One by one, the amateur competitors ran the course. For some, it was a breeze. Others found themselves facedown in the snow, victims of the trick course's two large jumps.

When Kaleb's turn was near, he was escorted to a waiting snowmobile, which would take him to the top of the course. He held on tightly as the vehicle revved its engine and took off up the slope to the starting line.

On the way up, Kaleb noted numerous places along the course where camera stations had been set up. At the top of the course, a small building had been constructed. Next to it, a thick red line was painted on the packed snow. An X-treme Compete crew member directed him to the building, where he waited as the competitor ahead of him began his run.

Soon it was Kaleb's turn.

He stood at the top of the run and stared down. He'd boarded the course many times with Amber over the past few weeks, but standing here now, with the crowd and the cameras and the pressure? He nearly backed down.

Kaleb forced himself to take a deep breath. He thought of Luke, and his nerves washed away. An airhorn sounded. Kaleb took another deep breath, whispered, "Be fearless," and began his run.

One of the most important things about slopestyle was accurately gauging the correct speed for each jump and trick. Kaleb hit the first element perfectly, executing a simple 50-50 slide along the railing to gain some momentum.

He moved quietly onto the second jump, landing perpendicular on the rail in a backside boardslide. This move was similar to the 50-50 slide, but Kaleb had to be sure his board was at a 90-degree angle. It took a lot of concentration, but Kaleb did it perfectly.

Then it was on to the third and final rail. Kaleb attempted a much more difficult move. He ollied into the air, twisted so he was facing uphill, and planted only the nose of his board on the rail in a frontside noseslide.

Far below, Kaleb could hear the crowd cheering as they watched the large monitors.

The first part of the course was over. Only the two large jumps remained. Kaleb knew exactly what he was going to do when he hit the first jump. He'd envisioned it in his head so many times.

As he launched into the air, Kaleb leaned back and snatched his board in an Indy grab to keep his legs tucked. The snow disappeared as he performed a soaring backflip. He saw snow, then sky, and then the powder returned. He let go of his board and landed perfectly.

Nailed it.

Kaleb let out a relieved breath. But his comfort was brief.

One jump remained.

This was it. His biggest move. One last chance to really wow the judges.

Kaleb hit the jump and went airborne. When the world had fallen away and he was weightless, Kaleb spun in a circle, grabbed the nose of his board with both hands, and pulled up his front leg. It was a move Luke had taught him — the 360 rocket air. The trick was his brother's favorite, the move Kaleb knew Luke would have performed if he were the one competing.

When the move was complete, Kaleb got his board back under him and hit his landing perfectly. Every cell in his body screamed with joy.

He threw his hands in the air. The crowd roared its approval.

"Wow, what a fantastic run by Kaleb Pearson!" the emcee shouted into her microphone.

Kaleb waved to the crowd, unstrapped his bindings, and scooped up his board. He scanned the throng of people for his family, found them — and stopped cold in his tracks.

Luke was no longer seated in his wheelchair. Instead, with the help of his crutches, he stood applauding.

Kaleb tried to contain his emotions, but like a dam bursting, he failed. Tears ran down his cheeks as he rushed over and grabbed his brother in a giant hug.

It was just like his dream.

No. Better. It was real.

"Great job, Kaleb," Luke said. "I'm so proud of you, little bro."

"Thanks," Kaleb said. "I owe it all to you."

Then Kaleb's mother and Nick joined them in one massive family hug.

A large electronic board located above the judges' stand recorded each boarder's score and ranking. Kaleb watched with anticipation for his score. When it finally flashed on the screen, it was enough to catapult him into second place.

"Woo-hoo!" Luke cheered.

Nick lifted Kaleb off the ground. As his stepfather set him back down, Amber fought her way through the crowd and hugged Kaleb fiercely. "That was so amazing!" she said.

Kaleb looked over and saw Luke, who winked at him. His cheeks flushed red.

As the next contestant's name was called, Luke nodded in the direction of the course. "That looked like fun," he said. "What do you say I join you next year?"

"That . . . that sounds just about perfect," Kaleb said.

They watched the remainder of the contestants navigate the course. Some were accurate but predictable. Others absolutely killed it, making the crowd — Kaleb included — gasp in awe.

With each contestant, the scoreboard was updated. Kaleb stayed in second for the first part of the event. Eventually, though, he watched his score drop from second down to seventh place.

That was okay by him. The competition was never about scores. It wasn't about winning. It wasn't about medals or plaques. It was about Luke. About the joy and drive and reignited fire Kaleb could see in his brother's eyes again.

Seeing his brother smile made Kaleb feel like the day's biggest winner, hands down.

CHAPTER 12

BACK ON THE SLOPES

"Come on, slowpoke! What's taking you so long?" Kaleb shouted jokingly. He smiled and looked back over his shoulder at his brother. Luke was about ten feet behind him, carving down the hill on his old snowboard. A huge smile was spread across his face.

"Don't get cocky, dude!" Luke shouted, laughing. "I'm coming for you!"

It had been seven months since Kaleb had participated in the slopestyle competition, X-treme Compete.

Since then, Luke's physical therapy had progressed by leaps and bounds. He now moved without the use of crutches. He had begun to walk and sometimes even jog around the neighborhood. Often, Kaleb would join him for these early-morning outings.

Recently, Luke's doctors had given him a special prosthetic to use for more strenuous activities like snowboarding and skateboarding. It was more flexible and allowed for more fluid movements.

Now, the brothers were racing down the Mother Lode, which was back in its original state after the X-treme Compete Tour.

Luke hadn't quite mastered boarding with his new prosthetic, but he was getting the hang of it.

Kaleb slowed, giving Luke a chance to slide in beside him. Together, they hit the flat area of the trail. When it dipped down again, they sailed into the air.

Kaleb twisted his body around in a flawless 520. Luke completed a frontside grab and stuck the landing.

"Nice!" Kaleb called as he and Luke coasted down the hill at breakneck speed.

When they reached the bottom, Luke was the first to ask, "Again?"

Kaleb nodded and the brothers high-fived one another, smiling. "Lead the way, bro," he said.

It was just like old times, the two brothers competing with one another, chasing each other over berms and moguls, and maneuvering down many of Ridgewood's trails.

They stayed out until the sun dipped behind the mountains, and Kaleb finally boarded side by side again with Luke.

His best friend.

His brother.

His hero.

ABOUT THE AUTHOR

Brandon Terrell is the author of numerous children's books, including several volumes in both the Tony Hawk 900 Revolution series and the Tony Hawk Live 2 Skate series, graphic novels for Sports Illustrated Kids, chapter books, and a picture book about trains. When not hunched over his laptop writing, Brandon enjoys watching movies and television, reading, watching (and playing!) baseball, and spending time with his wife and two children in Minnesota.

GLOSSARY

adrenaline (uh-DREN-uh-lin)—a chemical your body produces when you need energy or when you sense danger

amputate (AM-pyuh-tate)—to cut off a person's limb, usually because it is damaged or diseased

confidence (KAHN-fi-duhns)—a strong belief in one's own abilities

envisioned (en-VIZH-uhnd)—imagined something in the future

exhilerating (eg-ZIL-uh-ray-ting)—very exciting

incorporate (in-KOR-puh-rate)—to include something as part of another thing

rehabilitation (ri-huh-BIL-uh-TAY-shun)—to bring someone back to a normal, healthy condition after an illness or injury

strenuous (STREN-yoo-uhss)—requiring great energy or effort

treacherous (TRECH-ur-uhss)—dangerous

DISCUSSION QUESTIONS

1. Kaleb copes with his anger about his stepbrother Luke's injury by boarding down a course more difficult than he is prepared for. Do you think this was a healthy way to for Kaleb to deal with his emotions? Why or why not?

2. Do you think Amber is a supportive friend for Kaleb? If so, how does she support him? If not, how could she do a better job?

3. Why do you think Luke is upset when Kaleb changes the TV station in his hospital room to a snowboarding competition? Should Kaleb have known it would upset his big brother?

WRITING PROMPTS

1. Imagine you are Luke. Write a journal entry about coming back home, injured, and trying to rehabilitate. What is frustrating? What is encouraging?

2. When Luke tells Kaleb he will be going overseas with his National Guard unit, Kaleb is upset and worried. Write a scene in which Kaleb expresses his emotion once he is alone and back at home. What does he do?

3. Kaleb feels proud of himself when he completes the slopestyle competition, even though he doesn't win. Write about a time when you felt proud of yourself.

MORE ABOUT
SNOWBOARDING

Reluctant to share the slopes, it wasn't until 1989 that most **US SKI RESORTS** finally allowed snowboarders on their runs.

Still a relatively new sport, the modern-day snowboard was invented in 1965 by **SHERMAN POPPEN**. He originally called the device the "snurfer."

Most snowboarding and skiing **INJURIES** occur when athletes try to ride down a slope that is beyond their abilities.

SNOWBOARD CROSS is a speed competition that challenges riders to navigate through winding courses with narrow turns, jumps, berms, inclines, and drops.

Snowboarding is one of the fastest-growing sports. It has been a **WINTER OLYMPIC** event since 1998 and is embraced by extreme sports fans around the world. Read these facts so you can keep up!

Snowboarding's history is largely unknown, but many people credit **M. J. BURCHETT**, a man from Utah, with creating one of the first snowboards in 1929. He made it out of a plank of wood, using horse reins and clotheslines to secure his feet.

SLOPESTYLE events are fast and wild! The courses are often covered with obstacles called "boxes" that look like big, slippery tabletops. Another obstacle often seen is the rail.

In the **HALFPIPE** event, boarders compete on a U-shaped ramp dug deep into a hill. Competitors rack up points by doing jumps, tricks, and twists.

SHAUN WHITE is considered one of the world's best boarders. Not only does he dominate the snowy slopes—he's also a professional skateboarder.